CW00486549

Cinema

Of

Vampires

About the Author

Christopher Zisi is a horror writer residing in Fredericksburg, Virginia. He is the creator of the horror blog *Zisi Emporium for B Movies.* Over the past few years, a horror film review by Mr. Zisi has been posted on this blog every other day. The films discussed on this blog encompass most of the horror genre, including vampire, zombie, ghost, science fiction, big monsters, insect monsters, psycho killers, sea monsters, etc.

On May 30, 2015 Mr. Zisi retired from the Federal Bureau of Investigation (FBI). For 25 years, he was a Special Agent with the FBI and spent several years in the Baltimore Field Office working drug and organized crime cases. After being promoted to a Supervisory Special Agent, Zisi was transferred to the FBI's Training Academy in Quantico, Virginia. During his years at Quantico, he was sent all over the world (especially Asia) to instruct foreign police agencies interviewing and interrogation techniques.

In addition to his blog, Christopher Zisi published a collection of his horror poetry last year. In <u>Escaping from the Institute</u> he created 43 poems spanning much of the horror genre. His next book will be another collection of horror poetry.

Cinema

Of

Vampires:

A collection of Vampire film reviews.

By

Christopher J. Zisi

Forward

To date I have posted almost 600 horror film reviews on *Zisi Emporium for B movies.* The most popular ones tend to be the vampire films. The films which I review are out of the main stream and many horror fans may not have heard of them. For example, Tom Cruise's "Interview with the Vampire" would not make it on my blog. However, 2011's "Planet of the Vampire Women" was sought after and highlighted on the blog. Any film receiving an Oscar or achieving top 10 box office status, well, I ignore those.

In vampire films, several sub-genres exist. Traditional horror tales, love stories, morality fables, science fiction, and mysteries have all utilized the bloodsucker. Fiction writers and film makers have also created their monsters as very attractive men and women. The werewolf genre would have a hard time doing that. Eternal life is another gift given to the vampire, though in most of these films that follow, it is never attained. For all of the above reasons, the vampire is the most popular horror device, and has been for over 100 years.

This work is dedicated to the great people of Serbia. These hardworking and creative souls often reminded me, during my visit there, that the vampire legend was created in their great nation.

The Vampire's Coffin (1958)

Ariadna Welter is a stunning Mexican actress, and in 1958's "The Vampire's Coffin," she turns in one of the finest scream-queen performances you will ever see. Directed by Fernando Mendez, this is one of the best international versions of Dracula, tweaked to accommodate Mexican cinema. Complete with foggy graveyards, long dark and shadowy hallways, abandoned and ominous city streets, plus a dramatic and heavy spooky score, this film is a sleeper of vampire classics. In this film, as a nurse, Ms. Welter is an angel in white in much peril from our toothy fiend. As she returns to her career in the theater, she will finish the movie clad as a jungle goddess who may be doomed to be a vampire bride.

Many years ago, Count Lavud unsuccessfully tried to make Marta (Welter) his bride. For his unsuccessful efforts, our suave vampire got a stake in the heart. Some bad decisions lead to Doctor Mendoza (Guillermo Oreo) stealing the coffin from an old cemetery. The grave robber (Yerye Beirute) removes the stake from the fiend, and now Count Lavud has another opportunity to make Marta his betrothed. Doctor Enrique Saldivar (Abel Salazar, who also produced this work) saved Marta the first time, and now he must protect his pretty nurse from the current danger. Dr. Mendoza brought the vampire back to the hospital to experiment on it, but these types of experiments rarely work out well. Now Count Lavud is determined to have Marta...but it will have to be over Dr. Saldivar's dead (...or drained body).

As the body Count rises, and Marta is put under the his spell, Saldivar can't convince anyone a vampire is loose in his hospital. Valiantly Saldivar thwarts the vampire's best efforts, but Lavud is getting stronger and wiser. As Marta reports to the theater for her return as an actress/dancer, the Count begins to feed on actresses on his way to Marta's jugular. As our damsel debuts as a jungle princess, manhandled by natives on stage, Lavud plots her abduction and his evil marriage ceremony to her. The heroic Saldivar must put his life on the line, not only from Lavud, but from Lavud's evil servant in order to save Marta.

The last 15 minutes is a wild ride and will remind you of the action and music in those old Saturday matinee serials. Lots of cliffhanger type stunts concerning fangs, guillotines, torture devices, death defying fights, spears, and iron maidens are all packed into those last few minutes. Saving Marta from an eternity of vampire wifedom seems remote, Dr. Salvidar will risk everything to see that doesn't happen. Available on Netflix, see "The Vampire's Coffin," and enjoy the scares and thrills.

The Vampire and the Ballerina (1960)

Erotic and dark are two adjectives that best describe 1960's Italian horror film, "The Vampire and the Ballerina." Quirky is also a fitting descriptor. For example, when a troupe of sultry ballerinas find out a vampire is stalking them, they quickly put together an improv routine high on eroticism and ominousness which features the helpless damsels put upon by a dark force. What initially seems like a standard Dracula-theme plot, quickly takes a turn to add some neat mystery to the story. Heavy on beautiful, buxom damsels, and maybe a couple of shapely vampires, "The Vampire and the Ballerina," gratuitous and horrific, is a neat take on the vampire legend.

Our beautiful damsels arrive at an inn in a town where local babes have been bitten by a vampire. On their first night, the lovely Brigitte is bitten and turned by a grotesque bloodsucker. The next evening finds Luisa (Helene Remy), her BFF Francesca (Tina Gloriani), and Francesca's fiancé, Luca (Isarco Ravaloli) lost and finding refuge in an old castle. They are greeted by the sultry Countess (Brigitte Castor) and her apparent servant, Herman (Walter Brandi). When Luisa gets lost in the hallways, she is preyed upon and bitten by that grotesque vampire. The trio flee the castle, but now Luisa is under the spell of that vampire.

Suspecting that the Countess is...well...maybe a vampire, Francesca tries to warn the other gals. Knowing Francesca is on to them, the Countess, who may be a vampire, Herman, who may be a vampire, and that grotesque vampire set their sights...and fangs on the fair Francesca. Her tormentors have an ally; the beautiful spellbound Luisa also plots Francesca's demise. Just who exactly are the vampires, and what do they have in mind? Are there some spirited cat-fights in store for us in this film?

Heavy on gratuitous and erotic dance scenes, this film highlights some very beautiful actresses...and perhaps a hot vampire or two. Ballet fans may be a bit disappointed as our troupe more resembles a collection of dance hall damsels than the cast of "Swan Lake." With a few twists to the standard vampire film plot, "The Vampire and the Ballerina" is a terrific and atmospheric film which can be found on YouTube.

The Playgirls and the Vampire (1960)

"Raw Naked Terror" is the perfect tagline for 1960's "The Playgirls and the Vampire" (especially the Naked part). From Italy, director Piero Regnoli cast five very shapely actresses to play damsels in much distress. Much of the film has these vixens clad in see through negligees, or just plain nude. However, much danger our lovelies find themselves in, they always find time to rehearse seductive dance numbers or meticulously put on, or take off 1960s type European undergarments. In addition to all of the aforementioned frolic, we have a neat Gothic vampire tale set in a cool old castle, with a few well-placed twists at the end.

A bus carrying five sexy showgirls, their manager (Alfredo Rizzo), and bus driver (Leonardo Batta) is stranded outside an old castle after a flood. After hesitating, Count Gabor (Walter Brandi) invites the crew to stay at the castle. Gabor initially attempts to send them away, but after casting his eyes upon the voluptuous Vera (Lyla Rocco) he changes his mind. However, a warning ensues..."don't leave your rooms at night." Before turning in, our girls don some see through attire and rub their legs a lot, and then Katia (Maria Giovannini) decides to explore. Being beautiful means not having to obey the rules, but it also means drawing the prurient interests of centuries old vampires. Hence the fate of Katia, first killed. We soon find out that Katia's death, though temporary, was a case of mistaken identity, as Vera was the intended target of the fangs. Later in the plot, Katia will return as an undead, naked, and jealous bloodsucker.

Gabor warns Vera of a centuries old curse on his family and ancestors and implores her to depart. Vera feels a strange sense of belonging to the castle, and a love for Gabor. Of course Vera just happens to be a spitting image of one of Gabor's ancestors who died centuries ago. Reincarnated? Now Vera is stalked by the undead bloodsucker. With Katia now a bride of the vampire, her desire to share her fang-man with Vera is non-existent. Now Katia is also on the prowl to protect her turf. Clad in a very see through little thing, and a leather coat (which falls off quickly), Vera is running through the castle screaming a lot in much peril. Will Gabor protect her... or does he seek her jugular vein?

However playful this flick is, it is also stylish and suspenseful. The eroticism missing from American horror in this era, is piled high in Italian horror. The hard to find DVD is now available on Amazon. Though some of the vampire effects may be slightly cheesy, the seductiveness of the damsels is first-class.

The Slaughter of the Vampires (1964)

From Italy, we have a vampire tale which will appeal to fans of romance novels. 1964's "The

Slaughter of the Vampires" (aka "Curse of the Blood Ghouls") is equipped with flowery language, a big castle, a waltz in the ballroom, and a hunk prince-type fawning all over the vulnerable, buxom lady dressed in white gowns. Don't fret guys, this film has a really attractive leading woman, lots of vulnerable cleavage action, and some vampires. Directed by Roberto Mauri, probably for the benefit of his wife or GF, let us take a look a neat Gothic horror tale.

As our tale begins, a vampire (Dieter Eppler) and his babe vampire wife are fleeing angry townsfolk. The vampire gets away, but his wife is skewered with a dozen pitchforks. He gets out of Dodge and finds himself back at his old castle where he sets up his coffin in the cellar. Times change, and so do real estate deeds, as Wolfgang (Walter Brandi) and his buxom wife Louise (Graziella Granata) have moved in. On their first night they throw a formal ball and all the ladies are dressed in ornate ball gowns. Our vampire awakens and wanders upstairs and is immediately captivated by Louise's cleavage....er, beauty.

Game on, he puts Louise under his spell and bites her in her bedroom. She'll become his vampire bride. Wolfgang, clueless that he is, needs help. He fetches Dr. Nietzsche (Luigi Batzella) from Vienna. Yep, nothing new here for the good doctor. He knows exactly what they're dealing with, and begins a war against the vampire. He better hurry as everyone in the estate is in danger of being bitten, from the beautiful governess to the groundskeeper's little daughter. The hungry fiend, and his new bride set their sights, or fangs, on anything that moves...and has cleavage.

Gothic and melodramatic, this is still an enjoyable film during Halloween season. The women, living and undead, are stunning, and the men who protect them are handsome and over matched. Available on YouTube, if you guys want your GF or wife to watch a horror film with you, try "The Slaughter of the Vampires."

Cave of the Living Dead (1965)

1965's "Cave of the Living Dead" (aka "Night of the Vampires") is a chilling vampire story from, at the time, West Germany. This movie is shot in black and white and will remind the viewer of the silent classic "Nosferatu." Though not very original, the camera work, and the jazzy musical score make this a very effective film. An ominous old castle, spooky caves, shadowy streets, hounds howling in the distance, and plenty of vampires keep us on edge.

The plot: In a quaint, but superstitious village, seven attractive young women have died. The deaths occur between midnight and one a.m., and always during a power outage. The small town doctor classifies each death as "heart failure" (...no kidding). Inspector Frank Dorin (Adrian Hoven) is sent to the town from the big city to get to the bottom of things. He immediately meets Karin (Karin Field), the beautiful and statuesque assistant of the mysterious professor. She was hired by this professor to research blood at the professor's castle at the edge of town. During their first meeting, the power goes out and a beautiful barmaid (Erika Remberg) is turned into a vampire in her sleep (see picture below).

After getting nowhere with the local constabulary, or the town doctor, the Inspector visits the town witch who tells him of vampires, and equips him with weapons to battle these bloodsuckers. Frank learns that the caves at the edge of town also lead to the professor's castle. He accepts an invite to stay at the castle which allows him to romance Karin, and investigate his strange host, who arrived in town the same time the girls started assuming room temperature. At this same time, the barmaid rises from the dead and starts prowling around while sporting some new fangs. Unfortunately for Karin, she gets suspicious of her employer and now the barmaid (under the professor's spell) is seeking out her neck.

Will Frank be able to save Karin from the toothy barmaid? How will Frank explain all these supernatural occurrences to his efficient, German bosses in the big city? Is this movie an attempt to showcase a post-war metaphor of the evils that await a split Germany? Okay, that last question is only designed to make me seem intelligent... sorry. This is a creepy and atmospheric tale, and even contains some surprising nudity. Karin Field does a great job portraying the beautiful, but intelligent damsel in eventual distress. Though Hammer was creating lots of vampire movies during the 1960s, "Cave of the Living Dead" has more of a silent movie feel to it. See this movie, and don't sleep with the window open.

Maneater of Hydra (1967)

Go ahead, eat plants. Don't be surprised, however, if they decide to eat you. We keep them in pots, or a confined garden, but our plant friends may decide to roam, and eat. I guess that is only fair. We eat them, they eat us. One of my favorite Creature Feature films was 1967's "Maneater of Hydra" (aka "Island of the Doomed"). After all, the thirst for human blood spans all of nature. This film from Spain stars Cameron Mitchell in his finest performance.

After many of it's citizens were found with their blood drained, the citizens of Hydra fled. Fearing vampires, these scared townspeople left a weird Baron (Mitchell) as the only resident of the island. The Baron is pleased to be left alone. He is a botanist and scientifically engineers new species of carnivorous plants. Most of these green things feast on mice, except for the Baron's most treasured creation....a huge vampire plant which feasts on human blood. Six tourists will find this out the hard way as they pay the Baron a visit.

The man-eater goes right to work. After the tour guide is drained, a Sophia Loren look-a-like, Cora (Kai Fischer) is next. Cora is a loose woman with extra-marital sex on mind. Her search for it will not go well. Like the guide, Cora will have all her blood sucked out through her once stunning face. The Baron, unbeknownst to his guests, assists the plant in it's quest for human blood. As more guests succumb to the vampire plant, the fair Beth (Elisa Montes) and hunk David (George Martin) fall in love. Will the ever decreasing number of tourists figure out that their host plans to add them to a macabre buffet? Will the fair Beth be spared a horrible fate, or will her new hunk beau have to save her? Will the evil Baron prevail, or end up fed to his own creation?

Not a traditional bloodsucker, but our green antagonist is just as horrific. Perhaps predictable, this horror film benefits from a great performance by Cameron Mitchell as the demented and evil Baron. Slimy green things that capture you and suck you dry man not be a threat in our home gardens, but for guests of a mad scientist....be very afraid.

Countess Dracula (1970)

We have all wondered how smart (...or dangerous) we would have been in our college years if we knew then what we know now. In 1970's "Countess Dracula," Ingrid Pitt (as Countess Nodosheen) finds out. A Hammer Film based on the historical Elizabeth Bathory. In the 1980s I had the pleasure of having Raymond McNally as a professor at Boston College. He traveled to Romania and wrote a book about Bathory entitled "Dracula Was a Woman." Bathory bathed in the blood of virgins in order, she believed, to keep young. Sort of the Oil of Olay of the 17th century. Perfect fodder for a Hammer film!

The plot: As the film begins, a very elderly and cantankerous Countess Nodosheen arrives home after her husband's funeral. A chambermaid accidentally cuts herself while helping the Countess take a bath. The ever grouchy old hag slaps her and gets some of the maid's blood on her face. Miraculously, that area of her face changes into that of a young woman's face. Up until now, the Countess assumed she'd have to settle for the aged Captain Dobi. Enlisting the aid of her nursemaid, the Countess lures beautiful virgins to the castle where she kills them and bathes in their blood. After the baths, the old hag turns into Ingrid Pitt. How to explain this to her servants? She and Dobi assert that the Countess is actually Ilona (see picture below), her daughter. Ilona (Lesley-Anne Down), traveling home, is intercepted by Dobi's highwaymen and abducted. Imprisoned by a drooling semi-mutant, the beautiful Ilona is terrorized and pawed by this fiend.

No one in the town has seen Ilona for 12 years, as she was sent away to be protected from the invading Turks. With Ilona in captivity, the Countess can assume her identity. With her new youth, she loses interest in Dobi and romances the young and very manly Lieutenant Toth. Major problem! The blood baths do not last and she must continue bathing in virgin blood. Each time she obtains youth, the session is shorter and shorter, and when she ages again, she gets older and older. After going through the beautiful virgins, she settles for the homely virgins. With all the virgins gone, and a marriage on the horizon to Lt. Toth, where will she find her next victim? You guessed it ... a new peril for our beautiful damsel, Ilona.

As Toth accidentally walks in on one of the Countess' bathing rituals, he realizes that he is the object of a very diabolical plan involving the real Ilona. Will Toth lose his interest in older women and save Ilona? Will the Countess be hated because she is beautiful? The conclusion of this film is exciting, and the Countess' wisdom of the ages is tested against her need for and ability to obtain virgin blood. Ingrid Pitt is fantastic here. She died in 2010, on her way to an appearance at a horror convention in the UK. Her fame as one of the greatest "scream-queens" won her millions of fans, whom she always respected. "Countess Dracula" may be this Hammer-Glamour girl's best film. Not a victim needing rescuing here, but a stunning, powerful and ominous 17th century femme-fatale.

The Vampire Lovers (1970)

Upon her wedding day, Queen Victoria's daughter received this piece of advice from her mom, regarding the wedding night; "Just lay back and think of England." Similarly, Ingrid Pitt sought advice regarding her intimate lesbian scenes when she was starring in 1970's "The Vampire Lovers." Director Roy Ward Baker offered only this to his beautiful actress, "Just enjoy it." The eroticism hinted at in Hammer vampire movies comes gushing forth in today's selection. TVL is a perfect companion piece to Hammer's "Countess Dracula" (reviewed on this blog on May 4th), as both star Ingrid Pitt, arguably the best scream queen in film history.

The plot; During an aristocratic ball in Vienna, a countess (Dawn Addams) arrives with her apparent, niece Marcilla (Pitt). All the guys are checking out this stunning beauty, and in turn, Marcilla checks out all the buxom young ladies. In a suave scam, the woman pawns Marcilla off on a general (Peter Cushing), while she attends a sick relative. Perfect for Marcilla, as she is lusting for the general's daughter, Laura (Pippa Steel). As Marcilla is a guest in the general's mansion, Laura and her grow increasingly close.

Eventually there is a lot of intimacy and nudity associated with these two. Uh oh! Laura is getting weaker and paler. When Laura finally departs this mortal coil, Marcilla is nowhere to be found. What is found are two puncture marks on Laura's neck.

Marcilla pops up again, this time as Carmilla. We find out that this vampire is the last "living" descendant of the cursed Karnstein family (see my review of "Twins of Evil"). In a similar scam, Carmilla is taken in by the Morton's. Good news for our fiend, as now she can set her sights on Emma Morton (Madeline Smith). As Carmilla gets naked and intimate with Emma, and Emma's governess (Kate O'Mara), the general assembles a posse to end the evil once and for all. Will our heroic posse be in time to save Emma from an unspeakable evil?

This vampire's lust for beautiful young women is the draw for TVL. Pitt, Smith, Steel, and O'Mara are all beautiful in this. Peter Cushing, as usual, is terrific as the grieving father turned vampire hunter. As the 1970s progressed, these Hammer horror films began to increase the eroticism...which believe it or not... coincided with decreased box office revenues. In any event, this film will certainly please all Hammer horror film fans. The beauty of the glamour women of Hammer films has never been matched by the more contemporary actresses. Available on Netflix, treat yourself to what some may term a "guilty pleasure."

Count Yorga, Vampire (1970)

I first saw 1970's "Count Yorga, Vampire" at a drive-in movie theater in West Roxbury, Massachusetts, along with "She Beast" and "The Abominable Dr. Phibes." It would be almost a decade before I summoned up enough courage to watch another horror movie. There were three scenes in this film that had me screaming and hiding on the floor of my parent's car (I was only six). Directed by the late Bob Kelljan (Charlie's Angels and Starsky and Hutch), and starring Robert Quarry, this movie will give the kids nightmares.

The plot: Count Yorga, in his coffin, arrives by ship in Los Angeles, from Bulgaria. He is first seen conducting a séance with two young couples. Donna, one of the gals seeks to contact her recently deceased mother. Little does Donna know; her dead mom is now one of Yorga's undead brides (he has two). The séance is unsuccessful, but Yorga is able to hypnotize Donna, for later use. Meanwhile, Erica and Paul get their van stuck driving away from Yorga's place. During the night, Yorga knocks out Paul and bites Erica. Later that day, Erica displays some mildly anti-social behavior...such as trashing her apartment, displaying a desire to be dead, and eating her pet cat. Worried, Paul calls the promiscuous and boring Dr. Jim Hayes. A Van Helsing wannabe, the dullard gives the lovely Erica a blood transfusion, and calls the cops (who laugh at him). Later that night, Yorga pays the seductive Erica another visit and completes his task of changing her into one of his undead brides.

To be fair, L.A. is not Bulgaria, and Yorga gets a fast lesson on that. His first two brides are very voluptuous, however, when they wake for the first time in their undead state, they turn out to be lesbians, more interested in each other, than Yorga. With Erica gone, Donna, the two husbands, and the boring Dr. Jim Hayes head to Yorga's mansion. The plan: bore Count Yorga to death (I'm not kidding). When this doesn't work, the team returns the next night with wooden stakes, setting up a terrifying conclusion.

Count Yorga comes across as a horrifying and sympathetic figure. He is polite, classy, elegant, exotic, interesting, and very lonely in L.A. If he wasn't so evil and ominous, we might have been pulling for him. Judy Lang portrays Erica, and she is quite captivating on the screen. If you can, see "Count Yorga, Vampire" on a large screen with a quality sound system...and get ready for some sleepless nights.

The Return of Count Yorga (1971)

"Count Yorga, Vampire" may be one of the scariest films of the 1970s. In 1971, the sequel, "The Return of Count Yorga" hit the drive-ins. Robert Quarry reprises his role as the charming Count, and in a rarity, the sequel may be scarier than the original...and that's saying a lot. Before directing episodes of "Charlie's Angels," Bob Kelljan directed these two horror movies. Today we will examine the sequel, that was not afraid to push the limits on the taboo.

The plot: Count Yorga is back...don't ask how. As the film begins, women push out of graves, presumably victims of the Count. The un-dead babes then grab a little boy and turn him into a slave of Yorga. Cynthia (Mariette Hartley) works at a neighboring orphanage which Yorga has tabbed an all you can eat buffet. As Yorga visits the place, he bites the beautiful Mitzi (Jesse Welles) and falls in love with Cynthia. Cynthia's arrogant boyfriend, Dr. David Baldwin (Roger Perry), is very protective. That night, Yorga dispatches about a dozen of his wives to Cynthia's household. In a most chilling scene, the wives massacre Cynthia's mom, dad, and sisters in front of her eyes and abscond with the shocked babe. Now under Yorga's spell, Cynthia doesn't remember the attack.

In a horrific and heartbreaking scene, the lone surviving sister, Jennifer (Yvonne Wilder, also a co-writer of this film) who is also a deaf mute, tries to scream when she discovers her mutilated family. In a very forbidden area, Jennifer will later be killed by the little boy who is now Yorga's henchman. A little boy butchering a maternal figure in her sleep is unsettling today, never mind 1971. As David enlists the help of two cops (Ray DeLuca and Craig T. Nelson), the posse make their way to Yorga's mansion to find Cynthia. They will actually find more than they bargained for as Yorga's harem awaits their arrival.

Though a B-movie in every sense, including opening at drive-ins, both these "Count Yorga" films undoubtedly influenced some masters of horror. Stephen King and director Tobe Hooper most certainly used elements from these films in "Salem's Lot" which horrified audiences nearly a decade later. With a fraction of the budget as later, more famous vampire films, "Count Yorga" is definitely the scariest bloodsucker of the past 50 years.

Let's Scare Jessica to Death (1971)

As Norman Bates reminds us, "...we all go a little mad sometimes." No one knows this better than the protagonist in today's film from 1971, "Let's Scare Jessica to Death." Jessica (Zohra Lampert) actually went a lot mad, and landed in a psychiatric asylum. Like Bruce Willis, she saw dead people. But now she's better... or is she? The bad news, if she is better, what she is seeing will be more deadly than her insanity. Creepy to the max, patrons at 1970s Drive-Ins still have nightmares about a few of the scenes in this film. Filmed, and set in Connecticut, the cast of this film were driven from set to set in a hearse... you got to like that!

Jessica, Duncan (Barton Heyman) and his buddy, the proverbial fifth wheel, Woody (Kevin O'Connor) are moving out of New York City. The brilliant idea is that NYC is not conducive for Jessica's recovery, and an old, run-down farmhouse in the country will be. A few problems are immediately seen by the viewer. The family car is a hearse, and Jessica stops at all the cemeteries to trace gravestones. She should have taken up scrap-booking. Uh oh... even before they arrive at their new home, the voices start. Creepy ones, beckoning Jessica. She is the only one who hears them and she dare not mention them, for fear that she will land back in the loony-bin. She is also the only one to see the mysterious lady in white, who usually appears by the lake beside their home. Oh yes...the house they move into has a sordid past. A hundred years earlier the lady of the house drowned in the neighboring cove and the body was never found. Town legend: The lady is a vampire stalking anyone who sets foot near the lake.

The voices continue, and get more frequent. As they move into the new home, they find a squatter, Emily (Mariclare Costello). No worries that Emily is a spitting image of the woman who committed suicide 100 years ago. Jessica's visions continue, and she keeps them to herself. Only Jessica is suspicious of the townsfolk, as most of them wear bandages on their neck. Clue perhaps? As Jessica unravels, Emily makes a move for Duncan and Woody, further isolating Jessica from any safe haven. Bodies begin to turn up, but when Jessica brings help...the bodies are no longer there. Whatever is beckoning Jessica is emanating from the cove, which is the source of some of the most chilling scenes you will ever see. Is Jessica going insane...again? Are there vampires in Connecticut? Is Connecticut's inferiority complex to their neighbors in New York a source for insanity?

Absent sudden shock-scares, the imagery captured in this film will keep you awake at night. Everything about this film is unnerving including the musical score. However prevalent this film was at drive-ins, it is difficult to find now. Fortunately, YouTube has a good quality cut of "Let's Scare Jessica to Death."

☐

Twins of Evil (1971)

Two of the most famous Hammer glamour girls are Mary and Madeleine Collinson. These beauties, born in Malta and arrived in Great Britain as fashion photography models. Though their film careers lasted less than three years, Hammer's "Twins of Evil" from 1971 has developed a cult following because of them. In October 1970, Playboy featured the Collinson sisters as Playmates of the month, in one of their magazine's most famous spreads. Today Mary lives in Milan with her boyfriend and two daughters and Madeleine returned to Malta where she was happily married with three daughters. Sadly, Madeleine died in 2014. Oh yes.... Peter Cushing. I believe Cushing gives one of his finest performances as a religious zealot.

The plot: Gustav Weil (Cushing) and his merry band of religious fanatics roam the countryside looking for beautiful young women. Their lack of modesty naturally indicates that they are children of Satan prompting Gustav's morality brigade to burn them at the stake. How ironic, arriving by coach are Maria and Freida (portrayed by the Collinson twins) who have just lost their parents. Having grown up in Venice, their wardrobes are more revealing than Gustav would prefer. In his Puritanical uncle demeanor, Gustav welcomes his nieces by shouting "What is this plumage?" Maria is eager to show obedience to Gustav but Frieida is determined to rebel, not only in dress, but in taste of boyfriends. Freida immediately shows an interest in Count Karnstein (Damien Thomas). Karnstein is into the black arts and worships Satan. As Gustav continues to collect and burn the most beautiful women in Europe, Karnstein resurrects his ancestor Mircalla (Katya Wyeth). Mircalla, a vampire, then bites Karnstein turning him into one, as well.

As Maria tries to behave, she catches the eye of her music teacher, Anton. Freida sneaks off to see Karnstein and is welcomed by him, his girlfriend Gerta (Luan Peters), and Mircalla. Freida is very amenable to be turned to a vampire as well, which is bad news for Gerta. The newly turned Freida is given Gerta to play with and then eat...which she does. Upon Freida's return, Gustav discovers her vampiric condition, and has her arrested to be executed the next morning. Karnstein then abducts Maria and switches the twins, hence the zealots will burn Maria, allowing Freida to live as Maria. Anton to the rescue! Will he arrive before Gustav torches Maria? Because Anton does not believe that European babes should be incinerated, Gustav doesn't take him seriously.

A gory and fiery conclusion ensues. Saved by Anton, Maria rushes to Karnstein's castle to save her, now vampire, sister and is grabbed by the Count. Gustav comes face to face with Freida. Death, destruction, and dismemberment follow. Axes, spears, stakes, and plumage fly. Did the lack of tolerance and government sponsored diversity initiatives spell the end for witches and vampires in the middle ages? Did fear and hate of vampires' spell Freida's doom when she decided to be turned? "Twins of Evil" is a scary and entertaining movie. The Collinson twins may have been the most seductive of the Hammer glamour women. Peter Cushing's performance is fantastic! The DVD of this film is hard to find, but YouTube has "Twins of Evil" for your viewing pleasure.

Dracula A.D. 1972 (1972)

1972! The best of times. The United States had an ambitious space program. Canada beat the U.S.S.R. in a summer hockey extravaganza. Russ Meyer was still making terrific movies. The worst of times. Two ghastly individuals, Richard Nixon and George McGovern ran for the presidency in the U.S., giving our citizens a "Hobson's Choice." Pol Pot, on his way to winning a Nobel Peace Prize, was hailed by the international community as a peaceful statesman. Tensions in the middle-east threatened to bring about World War 3. Also in 1972, Hammer Films believed (incorrectly) that horror fans were losing interest in Dracula and attempted to make him a modern day menace. Hence, today's film, from 1972, "Dracula A.D. 1972."

100 years to the day that Professor Van Helsing died while killing Dracula, a London hippie-type, Johnny Alucard (Christopher Neame) taunts his pals to join him in a black mass. His motive is to resurrect Dracula. Fortunately for our wayward youths, a desanctified church is available and deserted. Fortunately for us the viewer, Laura (Caroline Munro) and Jessica (Stephanie Beacham of "Inseminoid" and "And Now the Screaming Starts" fame) are two of Alucard's friends. Oh yes, Jessica is the granddaughter of Professor Van Helsing (the grandson of the man who killed Dracula). This Van Helsing (Peter Cushing) is a doting grandfather and has continued in his dad's footsteps of studying vampires and the black arts. Unfortunately for Laura and Jessica, Alucard knows what he is doing. His intention is to present Van Helsing's great granddaughter to Dracula upon his resurrection, but an over eager Laura offers herself up for sacrifice first.

As blood spurts from an unholy grail, all over Laura, her friends flee in panic leaving the vulnerable and hysterical beauty all alone to face Dracula (Christopher Lee). Upon his return, Dracula drains her of blood and expresses his disappointment that Alucard did not provide Van Helsing's descendant as the sacrifice. When Laura's drained body is found, Scotland Yard gets involved and contacts Van Helsing. Realizing Jessica may be Dracula's next victim, Van Helsing assists the detectives in tracking down this fiend. After a near fatal meeting with Alucard, he locates Dracula. Unfortunately, after feasting on more of Jessica's friends, the Count abducts her and prepares her to be his next bride. A final showdown ensues in which Van Helsing must destroy this vampire before his granddaughter is condemned to an existence of evil.

Will our open-minded and non-judgmental hippies keep these virtues when faced with an eternity of sucking the blood of the living? Actually, these hippies are doing just that in a metaphorical sense in their "adult" years. Christopher Lee was furious that his contract mandated he make this movie. He apologized to his fans and expressed his embarrassment at being associated with "Dracula A.D. 1972." In 1972, this film might have been a disappointment, but today, a look back at 1972 through the eyes of Hammer Films is a lot of fun.

Vampire Circus (1972)

1972's "Vampire Circus" might have been the beginning of the end for Hammer Films. Bright red blood, beautiful women, intellectual heroes, and campy fun were the trademarks of Hammer vampire movies. Then came the 1970s, and the eroticism present in these films took on a more risqué flavor. However much movie makers claimed they were giving the customer what they wanted, the customer seemed to lose interest in Hammer at this time. In 2016, "Vampire Circus" may be the best vampire film that you have never seen.

The plot: Albert Mueller (Laurence Payne), while reading in the woods, witnesses his wife lure a little girl into Count Mitterhaus' (Robert Tayman) castle. A few problems here, Mueller's wife is now Mitterhaus' sex slave and the little girl is the Count's dinner. Oh yes, the Count, of course, is a vampire. Having had enough of their children being abducted, the townspeople, led by Mueller, storm the castle. In a bloody battle, the irate citizens apparently kill the Count. Mueller's wife, as the castle is in flames, runs back into it to be with the Count. Before he dies, Mitterhaus curses the invaders, swearing vengeance on their children.

15 years later and our little hamlet is enduring more problems. They have been quarantined. All roads leading in and out have been road blocked for fears of the plague. To their surprise, a mysterious circus arrives. A gypsy woman, played by Adrienne Corri (Moon Zero Two), is the ringmaster and features a black puma which changes into a man, mysterious twins (vampires), a tiger, chimpanzee, acrobats, and an ominous hall of mirrors. Then people start dying horrible deaths at the hands of vampires and hungry cats of prey. As the original posse which disposed of Mitterhaus begins dwindling, so do their children. Mueller must now protect his daughter Dora (Lynne Frederick). She is pure as the white snow. Ironically, Dora is portrayed by Ms. Frederick who was the world's most renown gold digger. She gained her fortune marrying men decades her elder, such as Peter Sellers and David Frost. Unfortunately, she spent too much of that wealth on drugs and alcohol and departed this mortal coil before her 40th birthday.

As the sultry gypsy woman leads her circus in pursuit of dear Dora, Mueller realizes that he must kill all of the vampires. Killing anyone in their way, the vampires devour the children at Mueller's school and abduct Dora. With Mueller pursuing, they all meet at the ruins of Mitterhaus' castle. Here a bloody final battle will ensue but not before the true identity of the gypsy woman, and the true destiny of the Count are revealed. Horrors, overt and implied, are prevalent in this film. Also, very erotic scenes, including a circus act featuring a man with a whip and a nude snake woman, are included. Creepy and disturbing, with a generous amount of that classic red Hammer blood, "Vampire Circus" will not disappoint. Too erotic for 1974? Perhaps. Hammer's glory would only last another couple of years. For today? You be the judge.

Baron Blood (1972)

Today's entry is a good one from 1972, Baron Blood. Directed by Italian horror icon Mario Bava, this film delivers good scares and teaches us valuable lessons. Joseph Cotton (Lady Frankenstein, The Third Man) has the title role, and Elke Sommer plays the damsel (an assistant museum curator) in distress. Mario Bava filmed this movie in beautiful Vienna (the setting for Joseph Cotten's most famous movie, The Third Man).

Okay! First the plot, then the ever important social commentary. An American college dropout dweeb boards a Pan Am flight to Austria. Great 1970s movie music accompanies this plane ride. His primary purpose in Austria is to research an infamous ancestor, the sadistic Baron Blood who was really good at killing people slowly with torture devices. Blood was knocked off over a century ago by a witch he ticked off. The dweeb's first stop is Baron Blood's castle which is being restored by Eva (Elke Sommer). Eva acts coy around the dweeb, and her wardrobes are always either tight, revealing, or low cut (or all three). Mario Bava does a great job utilizing Sommer's charm.

The dweeb and Eva end up at the same dinner party. Eva seems content in showing no interest in this dweeb. As well she shouldn't. She is beautiful, smart, ambitious, and will probably end up marrying royalty. Then the dweeb propositions her. The proposition? Let's sneak into the Baron's castle (it's dungeon to be exact), recite incantations from an old, cursed parchment, hence resurrecting the sadistic ancestor. Eva, against all logic, says, okay. The Baron is resurrected and Eva finds herself in more peril, especially when wearing slinky evening gowns.

The movie is exciting! Sommer and Cotton are terrific. Bava throws in a ton of blood. You will enjoy this slice of European, 1970s horror. You parents out there...no matter how intelligent your beautiful daughters are, keep a very watchful eye. If Eva can be seduced by this dweeb, there is no telling what miserable loser your daughter might decide to date.

Female Vampire (1973)

Okay, okay, okay! Yes, this film is Rated X. Before we can talk about it, we need to get a few points out of the way. ONE: The opening scene. Lina Romay is nude, except for some alluring leather boots. As the credits roll, she walks toward the camera...and yes, the credits end as her face collides with the camera. TWO: As she meets the farmer, and seduces him, she does bite him in...er... well, in the tally-whacker (...there's that word again). And THREE: "Female Vampire" might not be the most colorful title, but it beats "Male Vampire." So, with all of that out of the way, let's take a look at this 1973 Jesus Franco film. With our censors in mind, grab your [CENSORED] and let's take a peek at "Female Vampire."

Countess Irina Karlstein (Romay) is an erotic vampire. She bites her victims in their sex organs, males on their [CENSORED] and females on (or in) their [CENSORED], and then sucks their hormone juices. She has arrived on the island of Medeira, where her ancestors used to ply their vampirism. Karlstein is mute, and is approached by a reporterette, Anna (Anna Watican), clad in a pink bikini. After a short interview, Karlstein puts this inquisitive damsel under her spell, and eventually [CENSORED] and turns her into a love slave. Our final shot of Anna, is as she is clad only in white go-go boots, following Karlstein through the woods. In fact, most of the movie has our alluring fiend dressed only in leather boots and a leather belt. After sucking out [CENSORED] from her victims, she then has traditional (bad choice of words] sex with the corpses. This movie is Rated X and nothing is implied.

Dr. Roberts (Jesus Franco), the coroner cannot convince the police that a vampire is responsible for the rash of grisly killings. He joins forces with a blind Dr. Orloff (Jean-Pierre Bouyxou) to track down Karlstein. Karlstein is very hungry, and in one unforgettable scene visits a dominatrix. Succumbing to a whipping, Karlstein turns the table on the dominatrix and [CENSORED] a threesome. Then there is the Baron von Rathony (Jack Taylor). He is the worst poet in Europe and likes to trim his nose hairs. Rathony knows what Karlstein is. Nevertheless, what a way to go he figures and endeavors to arrange a tryst with our hormone-juice sucker. Orloff tells Roberts that tracking down Karlstein might be difficult, as the victims probably believe the ecstasy they feel in their final moments is worth death to them. Orloff' endeavors to converse and understand Karlstein, as Roberts has homicide on his to-do list.

Everything Karlstein does in this film, is not only done nude, but has penetration and orgasm in mind. She has sex with not only men and women, but also inanimate objects. In one weird scene, Karlstein longingly approaches a bed-post [CENSORED] and then with a cushion [CENSORED]. A final confrontation is inevitable, as Roberts enters Karlstein's bathroom, and finds her [CENSORED] lots of blood. I must give Netflix credit for recommending these types of movies to me. For your most guilty pleasure, I submit to you, "Female Vampire" (aka "La Comtesse Noire").

Salem's Lot (1979)

Between "The Texas Chainsaw Massacre" and "The Funhouse," Tobe Hooper directed a made for TV mini-series based on a Stephen King novel. I know, nothing says shocking horror like "made for TV" (can you detect my sarcasm?). The two aforementioned horror movies were frightening, but could Mr. Hooper deliver the scares on prime time network TV in 1979? Yes. The famed director delivered a relatively loyal adaptation of one of Mr. King's first novels, in very shockingly horrific fashion. The U.S. version, which we will look at today is over three hours in length, while the version that was released in the U.K. is 72 minutes shorter. The condensed British version should be shunned, as two of the scenes omitted are the opening one and the closing one.

David Soul ("Starsky and Hutch") plays Ben Mears, a boring writer. He's grouchy and doesn't have much personality, nor do any of the men in Salem's Lot. He arrives in town to do research on the old Marsten House. He believes the house is evil, and its history backs that up. Susan (Bonnie Bedelia, "Die Hard") falls in love with him immediately. Coinciding with Ben's arrival is the arrival of Mr. Straker (James Mason). Straker is a mysterious, and classy European who is opening an antique shop in town. Straker claims his partner, Mr. Barlow, will arrive shortly. Oh yes... Straker has moved into the Marsten house. Barlow does arrive...in a crate. The night he arrives, two children are bitten, and so is the town Realtor (Fred Willard). The bodies start piling up, and in some very shocking scenes, children vampires stalk other children. Ben tries to convince people that vampires have arrived in Salem's Lot, and they emanate from the Marsten House. Eventually, a high school teacher (Lew Ayres) and the town doctor (Ed Flanders) team up with him.

As Barlow and the new vampires go through town like crap through a goose, Ben and his ragtag gang of Van Helsing wannabes must act quickly. Beware, Barlow has the wisdom of dozens of lifetimes and is always several steps ahead of Ben. As Ben realizes that he will have to take the battle to Barlow, he convinces his gang that they must enter the menacing Marsten house. Oh yes, his most loyal follower is Mark (Lance Kerwin). Mark's parents were ripped to shreds in front of him by Barlow. Now Mark is a 16-year-old vampire hunter. Mark knows the score...he is a horror enthusiast. Uh oh, Straker and Barlow make a move for Susan... now the mission has a rescue component to it. Will Ben, over-matched and scared, be able to save Susan and keep his friends among the living?

Not much gore in this film, but it does contain very chilling scenes that will give you nightmares. Barlow is a very scary vampire. He sends children vampires after their parents and siblings and preys upon the character weaknesses of the townspeople. The U.S. version (183 minutes) is ominous, which Stephen King would have appreciated. The cast is great, the scares are effective, and the discomfort level is maximized.

Until recently, this 1979 adaptation of the best-selling novel was scarce in DVD format. If you have suffered through annoying teen vampires in modern TV and cinema, see "Salem's Lot," which reminds us that these undead vermin are stuff that horror movies are made of.

Fascination (1979)

Once again, with 1979's "Fascination," we examine a Jean Rollin film (See my review of "Killing Car" on my blog). If Hammer's "Vampire Lovers" (previously reviewed) was a playful film about lesbian vampires, "Fascination" is a risqué trek into surreal eroticism, a la Jean Rollin. Every single line or movement by Brigitte Lahaie (Eva) or Franca Mai (Elisabeth) oozes of seduction and want. This is a vampire story that will stay with you, not only in your dreams, but on your way to a cold shower.

The plot: Marc (Jean-Marie Lemaire) has just ripped off his gang after a heist. Pursued by his angry cohorts, he finds refuge in a mysterious, Gothic castle in France. As he invades the castle, he captures Eva and Elisabeth. These two women are lesbian lovers, so when Marc locks them in their bedroom, these two vixens engage in some pretty steamy sex with each other. They are also smarter than Marc, and get loose and begin a battle of wits with the handsome thief. The women conspire and Eva seduces him while Elisabeth gets the gun. As Elisabeth goes for the gun, she becomes most jealous when she notices that Eva is having too much ecstasy with Marc during passionate intercourse. Uh oh, Marc's cohorts, who he betrayed, bust in, and they want the loot. Eva brings them into the stables where she seduces them, and then neutralizes them. Eva is not only adept at sex, but also with a scythe. After seeing the two babes engage in homicide, Marc wonders what he has gotten himself into. Because they have lots of sex with each other, and him, he doesn't think too much about it.

Elisabeth is falling in love with Marc, and now Eva is jealous. Unfortunately for Marc, the two women have plans for him. It becomes apparent that they are keeping Marc at the castle, as they distract him every time he attempts to leave. The seductresses mention to him that some female friends are arriving after dark (clue). The sultry guests do arrive and prepare for a midnight ritual. So taken with the beauty and erotic behavior of the women in the castle, Marc ignores a myriad of clues that hint at his doom. As the after dark festivities get underway, Marc is lulled into a false sense of security as the women act as his sex slaves. He looks at them with lust, and the femmes look at him as a Doberman views a lamb chop.

The finale has some neat surprises. Does Elisabeth love Marc or Eva? What weird rite will occur at midnight? Does the street wise Marc have any hope of survival against these hungry lovelies? The scenes between Eva and Elisabeth are steamy, and so are the scenes with Eva and Marc, and Eva with her unwitting prey. Though Marc is warned by Helene (Fanny Magier), one of the guests, "Beware, death sometimes takes the form of seduction," he can't tear himself away from an evening of erotic delight. Available on Netflix, submit yourself to the spell of some very sexy vampires.

<u>Dracula's Widow</u> (1988)

Almost four years ago, Sylvia Kristel succumbed to cancer at the age of 60. The beauty from the Netherlands is still famous for three "Emmanuelle" movies in the 1970s. Her erotic performances in those films turned a lot of adolescents into temporary foreign film fans, as they were frequently played on HBO or other movie channels late at night. In 1988, she had the title role in Christopher Coppola's "Dracula's Widow." Christopher Coppola delivers a better movie than his uncle Francis did four years later when he made "Bram Stoker's Dracula." Though released in 1988, Coppola made "Dracula's Widow" in the style of the great Film Noir films of the 1950s, complete with seedy L.A. neighborhoods, dark alleys, cynical old police detectives, and an ultimate femme fatale.

The plot: Raymond (Lenny von Dohlen) owns a wax museum in Hollywood. Six crates from Romania arrive at his store (even though he ordered only five), as he is creating a Dracula display. Retiring for the night, two burglars break in and plan to steal valuable antiques. Unfortunately for them, Vanessa, Dracula's widow, pops out of one crate and drinks the blood of one of the perpetrators. Vanessa then heads to a seedy jazz bar and picks up a local L.A. radio personality. He takes Vanessa to a park to make-out, and Vanessa bites his face off and drinks his blood. Back to the museum she goes and meets the timid Raymond. Raymond is shocked, and Vanessa bites him, making him her slave. Under her spell, Raymond is cold to his girlfriend Jenny (Rachel Jones) unless he looks at her jugular vein.

The hapless Raymond chauffeurs Vanessa through the seedier parts of L.A. so she can nourish herself, while he settles for eating pigeons. At one point, Vanessa comes across some Satan worshipers as they are disemboweling a beautiful blonde. She joins in the ritual, and discombobulates all 15 of them after the ceremony. Crusty old Detective Hap Lannon (Josef Summer) shows up, with Van Helsing's grandson, and together they look for Vanessa. The corpses piling up all have neck wounds, and mangled faces. Hap doesn't believe in vampires until Van Helsing brings him to the morgue where the dead victims come to life as they are staked in the heart. Meanwhile, Jenny is distraught over Raymond's aloofness, and on

Vanessa's radar screen. Vanessa must kill Jenny, as vampires do not deal with jealousy well. As Hap and Jenny try to save Raymond, Vanessa gets deadlier.

Will Hap and Jenny save Raymond from Vanessa's spell? Will Jenny survive Vanessa's wrath? Will Vanessa blend in to the seedy L.A. nightlife? Fans of Film Noir will love what Christopher Coppola has delivered here. Sylvia Kristel is exotic and menacing, and Josef Sommer as Hap turns in a terrific Film Noir type performance. Don't waste your time with the 1992 Coppola vampire film, enjoy Christopher Coppola's "Dracula's Widow." This film is on Netflix.

Robo Vampire (1988)

I found Paul Verhoeven's "Robo Cop" a bit preachy and self-serving. Apparently the Chinese did as well, because the next year (1988), "Robo Vampire" was made in China. A cross between Lucio Fulci's "Zombie" and "Robo Cop," this film capitalizes on the gore and violence without pushing forth an agenda. Badly dubbed, and really corny martial arts only act to heighten the charm of this Asian cinematic achievement.

The plot: When you watch this film, don't worry about the plot... believe me... it'll come together eventually. Mr. Young runs an international heroine operation in the middle of Asia's "Golden Triangle." Vampires, who look more like Fulci zombies, are created by Young to guard their operation. The vampires hop like rabbits, hold their arms straight out, are adept at martial arts, and munch rather than bite. Young's people have created a super vampire which looks more like a hopping gorilla than it does Bela Lugosi. Unfortunately, the girl who the gorilla-vampire was supposed to marry, died. Now this unfortunate soul comes back as a ghost. She agrees to serve Young if he weds these two poor saps...which he does. Enough of this foolishness for now. Drug agents try everything to get to Young's jungle compound. Young's people kill two of the top agents and kidnap another, the sexy Sophie. Instead of killing Sophie, Young wants to slap her around a bit and subject her to Chinese water torture.

One of the dead agents is immediately converted into a robot. The robo-agent (actually not a vampire) then pursues the Young organization in order to free the helpless and vulnerable Sophie. The agency also hires a band of mercenaries to free Sophie from Young's tortuous clutches. Young dispatches his henchmen, who all run into gunfire, and the super-gorilla-vampire and his bride...the ghost, to fend off and destroy Robo Vampire. This all sets up an exciting jungle-combat conclusion with lots of gunfights and explosions, not to mention world-class martial arts.

Will Robo Vampire and the mercenaries be able to rescue Sophie before Young has his way with her? Will our newlyweds (the ghost and the gorilla-vampire) break away from Young and join the forces of good? This film is tons of fun and very violent. If you liked those badly dubbed Kung-Fu movies that used to play on Saturday mornings, "Robo Vampire" is the film for you.

Embrace of the Vampire (1995)

A few years ago my blog brought you the remake of 1995's "Embrace of the Vampire." While the erotic remake seems to be aimed at fans of "Buffy the Vampire Slayer," the original resembles a Gothic romance story with a vampire. Critics of the remake will quickly remind us that the original does have Alyssa Milano, often nude, to boast of. Fair enough. The more feminine version is directed by Anne Goursand.

Charlotte (Milano) raised by nuns, and a devout Catholic, is a virgin and always wears white. Actually, when she wears clothes, they are white, but in this film, that is sporadic. Oh no... she just happened to remind a centuries old vampire (Martin Kemp) of his long lost love. Our vampire was a French nobleman until three vampire nymphs had their way with him. Lucky him, he has found his true love on a college campus in the form of a 17-year-old virgin. Now, don't ask why, our bloodsucker has three days to bite her or risks losing her forever. As the vampire begins playing with Charlotte's mind, she begins to have weird visions and seems drawn to her nemesis.

As Charlotte's hunk BF, Chris (Harrison Pruett), realizes he is losing his virginal coed, the vampire seems a sure bet to end up with her. Leaving nothing to chance, the vampire unleashes doubt in both their minds about their love, and also Marika (Jennifer Tilly), to seduce Chris. The vampire begins attacking Charlotte's classmates, including the trashy Eliza (Jordan Ladd). Uh oh... Charlotte begins to explore alternate sexual norms, including a lesbian tryst with Sarah (Charlotte Lewis). With time running out, the vampire must make his move. Has Chris been sufficiently distracted?

Nudity galore, orgies, some gore, and some underage romance highlight this tale of the pursuit of pre-marital sex with Alyssa Milano. A bit different than the remake, the original "Embrace of the Vampire" is still a nice vampire story. Available on YouTube, treat yourself to an atmospheric, erotic horror/fantasy.

Night Watch (2004)

In October of 2015 I reviewed Day Watch which is the sequel to 2004's "Night Watch." Both films were directed by Timur Berkmambetov and filmed in Russia. Ambitious, action packed, gory, and playful, these films are fascinating. Sadly, the sultry Russian rock star, Zhanna Friske died recently (immediately after giving birth to her son). So again, let us look at an apocalyptic tale featuring vampires, shape-shifters, ancient prophecies, witches, and magic.

Anton (Konstantin Khabenskiy) is key in the battle between the light ones and the dark ones. Most are born into one of these camps, but Anton is special. He is an "Other," and chose his side. Uh oh, his son is also an "Other," and will be soon asked to choose. Evil forces in the form of a beautiful vampire have a head start and beckon Anton's son. To make matters more complicated, Svetlana (Mariya Poroshina) finds herself in the middle of Anton's pursuit of his wayward son. Svetlana has been cursed, and all who enter her life meet their demise. Svetlana's curse will eventually cause a decisive battle between light and dark which could destroy the world...unless Anton can find the source of the spell.

Anton must battle vampires and magic in order to save the world, and his efforts appear to be falling short. Help is on the way, the forces of light match him up with Olga (Galina Tyunina). Because of crimes long ago, Olga was turned into an owl. She is restored to human form perhaps with a chance at redemption. Anton would remark to her that he has never heard of that punishment... for which Olga informs him, "You have never heard of the crimes I committed." Quarterbacking the dark forces pursuit of Anton's son is the supreme dark one, Zavulon (Viktor Verzhbitskiy), who proves to be a formidable foe. His minions include a beautiful rock star, Alisa (Friske), who will duck out of a sold-out concert at his asking.

Like "Day Watch," this sounds so complicated. The key to understanding both these films is not to try to figure them out. By the final credits, you'll get it. The ending provides a smooth segue to the equally energetic sequel. Discussion of a third movie in this obvious trilogy may have been derailed by the all too premature death of Ms. Friske. Available on Netflix...enjoy the ultimate battle of good and evil.

BloodRayne (2005)

Lara Croft Tomb Raider, Resident Evil, and now three BloodRayne movies prove that video games transition well to the silver-screen. Many artsy-fartsy movie sites poo-poo the work of Uwe Boll (who directed 2005's BloodRayne), but when I see his name attached to a work, I'm definitely going to watch and enjoy. Say what you want about this movie, but I guarantee you that it is 100 times better than that Twilight garbage. The cast is also first class, including the stunning Kristanna Loken (Terminator 3), Ben Kingsley (Gandhi), Michael Madsen (Reservoir Dogs), Michelle Rodriguez (Resident Evil), Geraldine Chaplin, Meat Loaf (as an orgy obsessed vampire), Udo Kier, Matthew Davis, and Michael Pare (who appears in all three BloodRayne movies).

The plot: Kingsley plays Kagan, the most powerful vampire in the land. Many years ago he raped and killed a woman who bore his child. The child, Rayne (played by Loken) is half vampire, half human. Rayne has grown into a beautiful but maniacal carnival act. After nightly humiliation at this carnival, she succeeds in a bloody escape. She is hunted down by Kagan's henchmen, as Kagan realizes what a threat she is to him. She is also tracked by Vladimir (Madsen) and his people who realize she could lead him to Kagan. Madsen leads a vampire-killing clan. Rayne, in her attempt to track down and kill Kagan, finds out that Kagan desires an artifact which will give him supreme power. She steals this artifact, and now Kagan really needs to get his fangs on her. Vladimir and his people catch up to Rayne and they form an uneasy alliance in order to rid the land of Kagan.

The adventures along the way are bloody and most violent. Loken, as Rayne, looks really good with a sword and leather wardrobe. Her transition from lunatic circus act to determined huntress is compelling. Throw in romance and betrayal and a gory final conflict and you will never again be tempted to watch a movie with twinkling vampires. A+ for Uwe Boll, Loken, and the rest of the cast. Do not believe the bad reviews of this film. It is exciting and interesting. See the unrated director's cut.

Vampire Wars (2005)

I saw Vampire Wars (2005) on the Syfy channel, but at the time it was called Bloodsuckers. So impressive it was that I went to Amazon and ordered the DVD. The plot, again fairly original, a band of intergalactic sanitation workers is tasked with cleaning up the universe...not from trash, though. The V-San (Vampire Sanitation) crew is hunting vampire species. Of late, the different vampire species have waged bloody war against humans, especially the ones that are attempting to colonize.

This intergalactic crew is very successful and is made up of several salty veteran vampire hunters which eventually are led by Joe Lando (Special Unit 2). Lando is a terrific actor and assumes the role of the crew's leader. His inexperience is viewed, by the crew, as the reason their original captain met his demise during a vampire hunt. Because of its success, a very plotting vampire lures the crew to a remote planet where he and his other vampire friends plan an ambush.

The most appealing character is Quintana (played by Natassia Malthe, who played Rayne in the final two BloodRayne movies). She is half human and half vampire and her psychic abilities are key in tracking vampires. Like the Joe Lando character, her cohorts do not trust her, believing her vampire side is more dominant. She is clad in a nice black leather outfit, and you guys out there will be impressed. Tough as she has to be, and very equipped to kill.

The vampires are impressive. Several different species of them are portrayed, all hideous and able to do very gory things. My favorite were the oversized maggot vampires which explode out of the corpse they take over. The gore and Ms. Malthe's allure are the strengths of this terrific sci-fi/horror film. This is a movie not to be missed.

Day Watch (2006)

I have never been to Russia, but I have a great desire to visit. Moscow, St. Petersburg, and Vladivostok are all on my list of top 10 cities I must travel to. My blog has been remiss for not including films from this great country. So today we look at 2006's "Day Watch." The apocalypse, vampires, shape-shifters, and demons all wreak havoc on Moscow. Big budget, lots of great f/x, and an ambitious story are all assets to this Timur Bekmambetov film. This epic, filmed in Russia and Kazakhstan, runs over two hours, and throws a lot at us.

Anton (Konstantin Khabenskiy) and Svetlana (Mariya Poroshina) are kind of supernatural cops. These two, with some supernatural abilities, are tasked with keeping an eye on "The Dark Ones." The Dark Ones, and The Light Others are enjoying a truce in Moscow, though neither side trusts the other. If the truce is broken, the end of the world will ruin everyone's day. Each side has "Great Ones" who will keep them powerful. Uh-oh... Anton's son is just one soul... but he has joined the dark side. The beautiful Svetlana, Anton's hot partner, is destined to be a Great One on the Light side. Poor Anton, he desires a rekindled relationship with his son, and also a more carnal one with Svetlana.

Anton's son has taken up with the boss of the dark side, Zavulon (Viktor Verzhbitskiy). Zavulon has a vixen wife, Alisha (Zhanna Friske, who sadly died of cancer in 2015) who also has some neat abilities, especially with red sports cars. Alisha enlists the help of Anton's neighbor, who is a vampire, and together they assist in framing Anton for a murder of a schmuck from the dark side. Zavulon intends to use this frame as an excuse to start a war between light and dark, which will end the planet as we know it (...perhaps not a bad idea). Oh yes, Olga (Galina Tyunina) also tries to help Anton. Olga is a psychic, who at one point changes bodies with Anton. This body switching leads to one of the weirdest love scenes, technically between Anton and Svetlana....or is it Olga and Svetlana...you figure it out. All sound confusing? It is... until the end. When you watch this film, don't worry about understanding every scene. Before the final credits roll, you'll understand.

Will light prevail over dark? After centuries of fighting, has the line between light and dark faded? Will Svetlana and Anton end up together? Will Moscow survive? This epic feature has a comic book feel to it. "Day Watch" may look complicated, but if you just relax and enjoy the ride, all will make sense. Available on Netflix, enjoy this end-of-the-world epic from our Russian and Kazakh friends.

Rise: Blood Hunter (2007)

I first saw Rise: Blood Hunter (2007) on the Syfy channel, and was very impressed. Little did I know at the time, the 93-minute version which knocked my socks off was not the uncut version. I purchased the DVD, which contains the 122-minute (uncut) version. This version is in my top 10 vampire films of all time. Lucy Liu (Cypher and Kill Bill) and Michael Chiklis (The Shield) are both phenomenal.

The plot: Liu plays Sadie Blake, an investigative reporter, searching for a missing teen-aged girl. She gets too close to the truth, and the horror begins. The truth? A gang/cult of vampires are foraging through Los Angeles. Blake is a good reporter, and as she pieces the facts together regarding the teen's demise, she is abducted by the vampires and "turned" in a very erotic scene featuring Eve (Carla Gugino) and Ethan (Kevin Wheatley). Unfortunately for those two seemingly suave and sexy vampires, Sadie spends her vampire days not feasting on runaway teens, but murdering vampires in this cult. Armed with a mini-crossbow, she is very effective in exacting the ultimate revenge. Her crusade is momentarily complicated by Michael

Chiklis, who is the dad of that missing runaway she was originally investigating. They form an unholy alliance in order to wipe out these bloodsuckers.

One of the most uncomfortable aspects of this movie is watching Sadie, after being turned, gradually lose her human soul. In one scene, her family believes she is dead (I guess they were right), she visits her mother who is sleeping in her home. Sadie looks upon her mother lovingly, with sadness. Later, Sadie visits her again, this time she looks as if she wants to drain her mother of her blood.

The performances are terrific from top to bottom. The horror, blood and eroticism are rampant for all 122 minutes. Sadie's transformation into a vampire is dramatic, especially as her hunger grows for human blood. As she repels, not only the aggression of the vampire cult, she must also deal with Eve's carnal attraction to her. We the viewer are absolutely drawn in to the plight of Liu and Chiklis. See this film!

BloodRayne 2: Deliverance (2007)

One of my favorite modern actresses is Natassia Malthe. When not acting or modeling, she is active in philanthropic causes. Most recently, she raised lots of money and supplies for the earthquake survivors in northern Japan. This Norwegian beauty was featured in my blog for "Vampire Wars", and now we will look at 2007's "BloodRayne 2: Deliverance." Many of you may remember her as the femme fatale figure in LG's Scarlet advertising campaign in 2008...some of my favorite commercials! This Uwe Boll movie is the most playful BloodRayne movie, where the first one was the most intense, and the third one (also starring Malthe) is the most erotic.

The plot: Billy the Kid (Zack Ward) is raiding homesteads, killing parents and abducting their children. Neat twist, Billy and his gang are demented vampires. The last homestead they raided belonged to Rayne's (Malthe) friends and she tracks Billy to Deliverance. Deliverance is a small town which will get a railroad station soon. Billy now controls the town and Rayne is met with hostility immediately. When warned "...you don't know what you're dealing with," she responds "...that's fair, neither do they." Rayne, of course, is a damphere (half human/half vampire). This is explained in the first BloodRayne movie as Ben Kingsley (vampire) rapes Rayne's mother. After shooting a couple of Billy's men with silver bullets soaked in holy water and garlic, she is overpowered and put in jail. Fortunately for her, Pat Garrett (Michael Pare....who is in all three BloodRayne movies) rescues her just before her execution. Unfortunately for Rayne, she takes a couple of bullets, and is near death.

Garrett learns fast, and nurses her back to health by letting her drink some of his blood. Now Garrett and Rayne team up and put their own gang together, which includes a con-man preacher and a killer. Rayne needs to hurry; Billy has already started drinking the blood of the children. The gang returns to Deliverance and goes to war with the vampires, as Rayne breaks free to track down Billy for a horrifying confrontation. Billy asks Rayne to join him and gives her an ambitious speech about ruling the world, but she taunts him with "Big speech, little guns...you compensating for something, Billy?" As Billy begins kicking the snot out of Rayne, we the viewer are screaming (as if we are watching a WWE match) "Get up Rayne!" Who will prevail?

Will Rayne rebound and destroy Billy? Will Garrett and Rayne head to Tombstone next and confront the Clanton brothers? Uwe Boll, as in all three "BloodRayne" movies delivers a fabulously entertaining movie. He pays homage to the spaghetti western, and gives our protagonist the attitude of a seasoned gunfighter. Malthe looks great in her black leather coat and revealing garments...and of course two six-shooters. If you are not familiar with Natassia Malthe and Uwe Boll, definitely see the last two "BloodRayne" movies. Oh yes, Michael Pare is terrific as Pat Garrett!

Lesbian Vampire Killers (2009)

The immediate confusion in "Lesbian Vampire Killers" is what does the title denote? Is this a film about lesbians setting forth to kill themselves some bloodsuckers? Or is it a gang of Van Helsing wannabes tracking down vampires, who are also lesbians? The latter applies...though both the aforementioned story lines would have worked for my blog. In this

2009 film, we have lots of lesbian vampires, all sultry babes (...however undead, they are), and lots of gratuitous lesbian make-out scenes. Oh yes... we have a neat plot, that is interspersed with these alluring make-out scenes... so let us take a look at "Lesbian Vampire Killers."

A long time ago, a heroic baron ridded the village of Cragwich of the evil lesbian vampire queen, Carmilla (Silvia Colloca) Just before the baron be-heads her, Carmilla puts a curse of Cragwich, dooming every female in that village to lesbian-vampirism upon their 18th birthday. Present day, Jimmy (Matthew Horne) and Fletch (James Corden) are two losers looking to get out of town. They elect to go hiking in Cragwich. Also converging on Cragwich are four sultry coeds engaging in a history project to research the legendary Carmilla. Uh oh... they all have been lured to this quaint Cragwich cottage as an offering to a lesbian vampire coven. Lotte (MyAnna Buring) is the only coed who won't be ravaged and turned by the lady vamps. She teams up with Jimmy and Fletch to fight off the evil seductresses.

As Lotte (a virgin, by the way) and Jimmy (an ancestor of the Baron who killed Carmilla) fall in love, Fletch teams up with a vampire-hunter vicar (Paul McGann). We'll have some gratuitous shower action, gratuitous lesbian make-out action, and some gratuitous nude scenes...and then Carmilla's gang abducts the virgin Lotte. Carmilla wants her as a bride, but not before killing the Baron's descendant, Jimmy. As Jimmy and Lotte are strung up, the vicar and Fletch pursue a mad-cap strategy, which includes condoms filled with holy water, in order to free Lotte and Jimmy, and eliminate the lesbian-vampire scourge forever. Will the virgin Lotte be de-virginized by Jimmy or Carmilla? Will the baron's loser descendant man-up and be the vampire killer of the modern age?

All the actresses are stunning, and are quite alluring. This film is big on laughs, and still succeeds as a horror film. Gratuitous to the max, and offensive to those who insist on being offended, "Lesbian Vampire Killers" has a lot to offer. I understand a sequel is in the works, which is great, as Lotte, Jimmy, and Fletch emerge as a very appealing vampire-hunting trio. Directed by Phil Claydon, and starring some great actors, and beautiful actresses, enjoy this film.

We Are the Night (2010)

2010's "We Are the Night" (aka "Wir Sind Die Nacht") comes to us from Germany. It seems whenever we meet really sophisticated vampires, who have survived centuries, while accumulating the wisdom of the ages, they end up acting really stupid and getting killed. Will that be the fate of our four lovelies today? You'll have to wait until the closing credits for the answer to that question, but in the meantime, hold on for quite the roller-coaster ride. Machine guns, Russian mobsters, car chases, vampire carnage, love stories (all of the unhealthy sort), and eroticism are delivered in very loud fashion, here.

As the film begins, Louise (Nina Hoss), Charlotte (Jennifer Ulrich), and Nora (Anna Fischer) have just finished sucking the blood of every passenger and crew member on a Paris to Berlin flight. Louise, the leader, finishes off the last surviving stewardess. Big on adrenaline rushes, the trio pop open the cabin door and finish the flight on their own, letting the airplane crash. Meanwhile, Lena (Karoline Herfuth) is a low-life pick-pocket, running from the police. Tom (Max Reimelt), is on her tail, determined to arrest her.

On the run, Lena finds her way to a nightclub secreted in a Berlin park. Louise, who runs the joint, is fixated on Lena's desperation and allows her in. After attempting to seduce Lena, Louise bites her, changing her into a bloodsucker. With much angst and pain, Lena becomes a vampire and at first enjoys the apparent immortal life. Louise has intimate intentions for young Lena, but Lena is not a lesbian. Lena is sweet on Tom, even though he seeks to put cuffs her. The, now quartet of vampires, live the high life. They drive Lamborghinis, shop at exclusive malls, drink lots of blood, and hang around in bikinis and party dresses.

As Tom continues his pursuit, Louise also continues her's. Lena rejects intimacy with Louise which causes some difficulties. First, Charlotte becomes jealous, as she used to be Louise's lover. Second, Louise realizes Tom's continued existence makes a relationship with Lena impossible. Oh yes, Tom is actually a great cop and is able to locate these vampire femmes. With the full force of SWAT teams, the cops move in. Thanks to some nifty machine-gun work by Charlotte, the femmes escape, and an all-out war is now in progress between the police and the vampires. The immortal vamps prove to be anything but immortal. As casualties mount, Louise becomes unreasonable and impulsive, putting Tom and Lena in mortal danger.

Is there a future for Tom and Lena? How will Louise ultimately handle rejection? However lost Lena seemed, Louise never figured she had a human side. Now immortal, Lena finally begins to appreciate her humanity (...though she is no longer human). This is a loud, bloody, stylistic vampire story. Our four vamps are alluring and dangerous. However much a love story "We Are the Night" is, it is mostly an action-packed horror film. Available on Netflix, enjoy these four sexy monsters this Halloween season.

BloodRayne: The Third Reich (2011)

Today's feature is the third, and most erotic, BloodRayne movie. Check out the previous pages for the first two. In 2011's "BloodRayne: The Third Reich," our favorite damphere (half woman, half vampire) takes on Hitler's army at "the eastern front of the apocalypse." Filmed in

Croatia, in addition to Natassia Malthe as Rayne, this film is graced with some fine supporting performances. Michael Pare is terrific as the evil Commandant Brand, and Clint Howard as Dr. Mangler (a Dr. Mengele figure). Most notable is Safiya Kaygin as Svetlana, a prostitute that betrays Rayne. Also, stay tuned to the final credits to hear Safiya sing "Never Let You Down," or find her singing this on YouTube.

The plot: A Nazi train carrying Jews to a death camp is attacked by the resistance and Rayne. The resistance wants weapons and Rayne wants to kill Nazis. The attack is a success, apparently. Rayne chases Commandant Brand into a boxcar and impales him with a metal rod. As she does this, she then drains him of blood at the same time a Nazi soldier shoots her in the back, thus allowing Brand to ingest some of her blood. Unbeknownst to Rayne, Brand comes back to life as a Nazi damphere. Brand earns the attention of Dr. Mangler, who is summoned by Brand to coach him through his transition to the life of a bloodsucker. Mangler and Brand then realize they need to capture Rayne and bring her to Berlin, feed Hitler her blood, thus making Hitler immortal. On the way, Brand bites lots of soldiers, creating a vampire army.

At first Rayne is hesitant to join forces with the resistance, but she gets real sweet on Nathaniel (Brendan Fletcher), their dashing young leader. The resistance is quite capable with a dedicated core and a genius babe named Magda (Annette Culp) who can crack German codes... unfortunately, Brand captures her and turns her into one of the undead. Uh oh... Brand is now a damphere and his ability to hunt them down is maximized. Rayne is hiding out as the manager of a brothel, but when a jealous prostitute, Svetlana, realizes that Rayne's presence will bring heightened awareness from the Nazis, she goes to Brand and rats her out... then Brand turns her into a vampire. It should be pointed out that the scenes with Rayne in the brothel lead to some very erotic moments in this film. Brand, and his undead army are able to ambush the resistance and capture Rayne and Nathaniel. Once captured, Brand hangs Rayne up, feasts on her blood, making him really powerful, and allows Mangler to experiment with her.

Rayne and her soon to be lover, Nathaniel, are put on a truck caravan for Berlin. As Rayne regains consciousness, she and Nathaniel share some passion, but not before Nathaniel takes some cautionary steps. His caution may suggest that he has been intimate with vampire's before. The erotic scenes in the brothel, and Rayne's steamy love scene with Nathaniel will probably only appear in the unrated director's cut DVD. With a small group of resistance fighters on the Nazis tail, will Rayne and Nathaniel be able to escape and overpower the evermore powerful Brand? If you, like me, enjoyed the first two BloodRayne flicks, this one will have you cheering. Natassia Malthe's performance is perfect, as a beautiful damphere with attitude. Of course the gore is maximized, especially as Mangler conducts his experiments. If you feel like viewing an entertaining movie, don't waste your time with Twilight films, see "BloodRayne: The Third Reich."

<u>Priest</u> (2011)

Priest hit the movie screens in wonderful 3D back in 2011. As with most movies that I go ape over, not many people went to see it. Sure it was a flawed movie...as if "Gravity" and "Captain Phillips" are not! Unlike any Diane Keaton movie, this one had scary vampires, a lot of guns, futuristic motorcycles, old steam engine-trains, an old-western town, and some monsters. For those of you bent on avoiding Disney's "Frozen" this holiday season, get the Priest DVD!

The plot: A post-apocalyptic wasteland in the middle of nowhere is dotted with a futuristic city, run and protected by the Church. Walls surround this cramped, dark city, which protect them from monstrous vampires that roam the wastelands in packs. The Church and the vampire hordes are in a form of détente, or at least the Church says so. A group of militant priests with superior fighting/killing talents, who used to war with these vampires, have been ordered to stand down by the Church.

Paul Bettany is one of these priests. When his kinfolk are slaughtered by a vampire horde, he appeals to the Church to allow him to hunt the aggressors. The Church refuses, wanting to believe peace is possible in their time. Bettany disobeys and takes his guns and super motorcycle and starts the hunt. He is joined by a priestess (Maggie Q) and a cop named Hicks. As these three exact revenge, Bettany realizes that the vampires are organized and led by his old colleague who has been turned.

Priest has some nice (albeit brief) subplots. Bettany must resist the attraction he and Maggie Q share towards each other. He must also come to grips with the fact that his disobedience to the Church will have consequences. Most fascinating, however, is the conflict of serving the Church and serving God. Bettany chooses God.

Bettany, Maggie Q, and Karl Urban (as the vampire leader) all do fine jobs. The mix of old-west sets with futuristic city sets is kind of fun. Definitely 90 minutes of fun.

Planet of the Vampire Women (2011)

Made for $25,000 in a warehouse in Sacramento, 2011's "Planet of the Vampire Women" is a much better film than any of the "Star Wars" films. Primarily, every babe in this film is hotter than any women in the "Star Wars" films. A brief summary of this feature...space babes, often nude, and often covered in blood, fighting bloodsucking beauties. Mutant creatures, giant space insects, vampires, and doomsday bombs will play havoc with some sexy space pirates...who could ask for more?

A group of space pirates robs an intergalactic casino. Unfortunately, the hit got violent and a lot of blood was splattered, usually over nude women. Captain Richards (Paquita Estrada) leads our babe pirates and commands their ship on a getaway romp. Her crew consists of first mate, and former marine, Ginger (Liesel Hanson) ... a pleasure clone, Astrid (Stephanie Hyden) ...Automatic Jones (Keith Letl), a cyborg...Pepper Vance (Ashley Marino) ...Miranda (Danielle Williams), a junkie biker chick...and a few more.

Pursuing them is cop, Val Falco (Jawara Duncan). Both Falco and our gals crash land on a mysterious moon where Cpt. Richards is turned into a vampire by a mysterious beam.

Richards then starts biting the babes on her crew and flees the ship. Falco and the gals team up to look for Richards and some missing babes. As Astrid and Falco fall in love, and to Astrid's demise, let their guard down, the vampires pick off the girls one by one. As some sultry space babes get killed by monsters or turned into vamps, Falco and the surviving babes learn the secret of this barren moon. Now our survivors race against a doomsday clock to see to the destruction of the lady vamps, and prevent them from travelling to Earth.

Will our great looking protagonists survive this horror? Shouldn't pleasure clones be a more often used plot device in modern science fiction? Will Earth babes be spared the carnage our femme-pirates are enduring? This film, directed by Darin Wood, has more eroticism and pleasure than Mario Bava's "Planet of the Vampires." For an alluring and fast paced horror/action/sci-fi epic, enjoy "Planet of the Vampire Women," available on YouTube.

Kiss of the Damned (2012)

Everything about 2012's "Kiss of the Damned" exudes Euro-horror. Stylish, elitist, classical music, sipping expensive wine instead of Pabst Blue Ribbon, accents, manners, and tasteful lingerie indicate this movie has an air of sophistication about it. Filmed in New York, writer and director Xan Cassavetes does a masterful job keeping her film relevant to the widest range of viewers. In addition to very attractive characters, she even throws in a scene where Elvis Presley's real life granddaughter (Riley Keough) is drained of blood by the most sophisticated of bloodsuckers.

As our story begins, Djuna (Josephine de la Baume) lives alone in a Long Island mansion. She translates poetry for a living, and watches VHS tapes of old love stories. She is a vampire, and for the most part stays away from humans. Her life gets complicated when she meets Paolo (Milo Ventimiglia) while returning tapes to the video store. They fall in love, and he ends up back at her mansion. She confesses her vampirism to him and tells him they could never be together. At first she told him she had a rare skin condition and could not go out in daylight...which guy has not heard that line before? She proves it to him by having him chain her to the bed while she grows her teeth. This turns him on, and he allows her to change him into a vampire so they can be with each other forever. The transition is smooth as Djuna creates a home office for Paolo (a semi-successful screenwriter) in the mansion. The two sip wine or blood together, have a lot of sex, and do all sorts of sophisticated things together. Uh oh...a surprise visitor. Mimi (Roxanne Mesquida) arrives and announces she is staying a week. Also a vampire, hardly sophisticated, Mimi is on her way to Phoenix to go to a vampire rehab because her thirst for blood has gotten too severe. After all, the first step to wellness is admitting you have a problem, for this we need to applaud Mimi.

Mimi and Djuna do not get along. Mimi is a semi-Goth who is into partying and threesomes, and biting any guy who comes onto her. Her free will alarms Djuna as she believes Mimi's behavior will bring undue attention to the secret vampire community. As impulsive as Mimi is, she might be the smartest bloodsucker this side of the sod. She continues partying, and brings some of her victims back to the mansion for orgies before eating them. She even is able to seduce Paolo in the shower. The queen of the vampires is even victimized by Mimi. Xenia (Anna Mouglalis), an actress, is determined to send Mimi to Phoenix, but Mimi wants the beautiful life in New York City. Taking advantage of every vampire's hunger, Mimi strategically places Elvis Presley's granddaughter in Xenia's apartment at feeding time, and Xenia can't resist. To cover up this embarrassing lack of judgment, Xenia enlists Mimi's help. As Djuna and Paolo go to elite vampire parties and discuss human-vampire relations, Mimi plots.

For us the viewer, even though Mimi is the villain, we kind of cheer for her. Djuna, Paolo, and Xenia would have nothing to do with us... but Mimi? Mimi seems like the sort who would have a Moosehead or Blue Moon with us...and then drink our blood. What is Mimi's overall plan? Will Djuna and Paolo ever loosen up? As the final 30 minutes hit, subtle twists occur which cast doubt on the sophistication and refinement of Djuna. Is Mimi really the evil one?

The ending is unusual but satisfying. The acting is terrific and the musical score is truly outstanding. Xan Cassavetes writing and directing is magnificent. See "Kiss of the Damned" and feel free to have Heineken or Hoegaarden with it to enhance the European flavor of this work.

Argento's Dracula (2012)

Unlike 1992's "Bram Stoker's Dracula" (directed by Francis Ford Coppola), 2012's "Argento's Dracula" is actually a good movie. Rutger Hauer is a much better Van Helsing than Anthony Hopkins, and mercifully, Winona Ryder is not in the Dario Argento version. In Coppola's version, Gary Oldman (a fine actor) is a horrible Dracula, but in Argento's version, Thomas Kretschmann turns in a fascinating performance. What makes Kretschmann's portrayal so alluring? His Dracula seemed a cross between Bela Lugosi and the Governor from "The Walking Dead." Filmed in 3D, with an over-the-top musical score, "Argento's Dracula" is a lot of fun and very atmospheric.

The plot is typical of Dracula movies. As the film begins, Tanja (Miriam Giovanelli) violates a myriad of rules which B Movie fans know. She sneaks out of her house against her mother's wishes, meets a married man in a barn, has pre-marital sex with him, throws away her cross pendant, believes her paramour when he tells her that noise outside was just the wind...and before you know it... she is one of Dracula's brides. Meanwhile, Dracula summons Jonathan Harker to his castle to catalog his books. With Lucy (Asia Argento) already under his spell, Dracula's real goal is to make Mina Harker (Maria Gastini) his bride. Believing Mina is the reincarnation of his wife, Dracula uses Tanja and Lucy as pawns to lure Mina. The Governor...I mean Dracula is manipulative, charming, and smarter than anyone in the town. He can also take the form of an owl, wolf, rat, fly, roach, and praying mantis. If you hold your breath long enough, you can almost see an eye-patch on his face.

With Lucy gone... or undead, and her husband Jonathan missing, Mina searches for answers. Enter Van Helsing (Hauer). Van Helsing is all business as he goes through Dracula's brides and sycophants like crap through a goose. As Dracula succeeds in drawing Mina to his castle, Van Helsing heads there, well-armed, with garlic, silver bullets, a wooden stake, and crosses. Mina is no match for Dracula's hypnotic charm, and seems willing to succumb to his wishes. Will Van Helsing arrive in time to save Mina? Will Rick, Glenn, and Maggie...er...never mind.

While the 1992 Francis Ford Coppola version of Dracula wasted our time, Argetno's effort refreshingly paid homage to the real Bram Stoker work and also to Bela Lugosi who was Dracula in 1931. Some of Lugosi's most famous quotes, such as "...children of the night...what music they make," are included in this film. As for the acting, Rutger Hauer is always terrific, and Miriam Giovanelli is radiant as a very jealous bride of Dracula. As for "The Walking Dead" fans, it will be difficult not to call this movie "Argento's The Governor."

<u>Young Blood: Evil Intentions (2012)</u>

.... or one might term 2012's "Young Blood: Evil Intentions" as the anti-"Twilight" movie. No cool, twinkling teenagers who have graced high schools for generations. No centuries old central European royalty. No sophisticated recluses dwelling in mansions. Nope. In this film we have real people that actually look like our neighbors. Directed, written, and produced by Mat and Myron Smith, today's blog entry gives us a vampire story resembling how "Twilight" might have looked if Troma made it. Not a Troma film, but our buddy Lloyd Kaufman appears as a TV anchorman, in a very dramatic role. Filmed in Martinsville, Virginia (NASCAR-land) YBEI is a horror story, a satire, social commentary, and a comedy.... but it's default is all horror.

The movie begins at Anastasia's (Autumn Ward) birthday party. Lots of friends and family converging on a roller skating rink to celebrate this day, but it is ruined by the girl's abusive stepfather to be, Dale (Myron Smith). Once home, Anastasia's older sister, Anavey (Zoe Cox) takes her for a walk in the park. However strange Anavey is, we all know someone like her. The quasi-Goth Anavey, a vampire, then bites her reluctant sister on the neck, turning her into a bloodsucker. Anavey has a plan. She desires to turn all the children in her town into these fiends and then kill all the adults. Why such the hatred for adults? It doesn't take Freud to figure this one out. The girls' mother (Rebecca Kidd) is shacked up with an abusive Dale...who is appropriately clad in a wife-beater undershirt. Dale beats their mom, and also Anavey. After biting Anastasia, Anavey orders her to kill their grandmother (Brett R.M. Smith) in order for the transformation to be complete. This killing delivers much comedy...in a dark sort of way, of course.

As Dale gets more abusive, the girls kill more, all the while converting all the children in their school into vampires. The local church begins to hold anti-vampire rallies. Protesters will hold signs saying clever stuff like "Let Them Eat Stake." Mat and Myron Smith throw in lots of biting commentary regarding what violent adults, and broken homes can turn our children into. However, the commentary doesn't end there. Every institution in working class suburbia

receives attention from our film makers.
Teachers and parents meet horrible fates, and
our children turn more evil. However dark
Anavey is, it is obvious Anastasia has good in her.
As Anastasia's doubts about vampire culture
mount, Anavey begins growing suspicious of her
little sister's loyalty. Uh oh! Is it too late for
Anastasia?

Autumn Ward is absolutely FANTASTIC! Though
the adults are portrayed as out of touch and one
dimensional, we the viewer must realize that is
how the children see them. Kaufman (pictured
above) is his typical boisterous self, and presents
newscasts as only he could. However comedic
and satirical this film is, be warned, when it ends
there is no doubt we have just seen a horror film.
Kudos to Mat and Myron Smith for making a film
that is perfect for this Halloween season.

Embrace of the Vampire (2013)

Many of you who endured "The Black Swan"
claimed to have liked it, only to appear
sophisticated. Point of fact, it wasn't a horrible

movie, but ballet is not your thing, and Natalie Portman seemed moody and strange. Today's entry, 2013's "Embrace of the Vampire" is the film for you. It is the "The Black Swan" with vampires and slayers instead of ballet dancers.

The plot: Charlotte (Sharon Hinnendael) has just arrived at North Summit College, located in the mountains of British Columbia. She has no parents, and is on a full scholarship for fencing. Apparently NSC is a powerhouse in women's fencing, as they have about 40 babes on the squad, and are coached by a handsome Professor Cole (who is probably a vampire, and played by Victor Webster). Charlotte is informed by a weirdo in a coffee shop that she is the latest in a long blood line of vampire slayers, and she has arrived at NSC to kill some vampire. Clean cut Charlotte reacts to this information as many of us would, by behaving badly, neglecting academics, drinking, and trolling for boy or girl friends.

Realizing she must now watch her back, Charlotte must defend against naughty coeds, too smooth boyfriends, a faculty advisor who is afraid of light, and gory hallucinations. Worst of all, her English Literature professor and coach is a

300-year-old vampire who wants to turn her into one. Will she maintain a GPA worthy of a full scholarship? Will her fencing abilities be enough to fend off bloodsuckers? Will North Summit College win their sixth women's college fencing title?

This is the best fencing movie in the last 20 years! Fans of vampire movies will enjoy this film. The unrated DVD copy contains a lot of gore; thus this film is not for the squeamish. Forget "The Black Swan" and see "Embrace of the Vampire."

The Stranger (2014)

In a mountain town reminiscent of the one in "Twilight" comes a mysterious stranger. Unfortunately, there'll be no twinkling and games, rather gory carnage and death. From producer Eli Roth comes 2014's "The Stranger," an unusual vampire tale set in the fictional town of Grey Mountain but shot in Chile. Grim and creepy, this film starts with a pall of dread and proceeds to cascade downward as our visiting vampire proves that he cannot gel with the society of the living.

Martin (Cristobal Tapia Montt) arrives by sea one night. He is looking for his wife, Ana (Lorenza Izzo). The two split when Martin tried a murder/suicide (usually a relationship buster) thing as he realized Ana could not control her urge for human blood. Interrupted by a gang of the living, Ana escaped. He finds his old house occupied by Monica (Alessandra Guerzoni), a nurse, and her son Peter (Nicolas Duran). Peter tells him Ana is buried in the graveyard. Martin departs, heartbroken, and is quickly pummeled by a gang of youths. Peter saves him and brings him back to his house where Monica tries to administer first-aid. Peter warns her to stay away from him, as his blood will kill her. Uh-oh, the thugs set their sight on Peter, and they beat him up, but Martin returns the favor and dispatches them.

The town cop (Luis Gnecco) now has Martin and Peter in his cross-hairs, as the head thug, Caleb (Ariel Levy) is his son. The cop tortures Peter and burns him beyond recognition. Once again, Martin to the rescue as his blood is used to heal Peter. Now the cop is really mad and will stop at nothing to kill Peter and Martin. We are let in on the backstory of Ana and her death. No spoilers here, but we understand why Martin is hanging around. As Martin tries to stay in the shadow (...this never works), bloody carnage awaits a lot of innocent people. Too late to slip away quietly, Martin and Peter will have to confront their tormentors. Oh yes, Caleb is back...and he isn't quite human...or sympathetic to the ones who put him in the hospital.

Directed masterfully by Guillermo Amoedo, "The Stranger" is a perfect vampire film for those who thought the genre could give us nothing unique anymore. Not the feel good movie of the decade, and invading certain taboos, this Eli Roth produced film will surely please those that love their horror dark. Available on Netflix, enjoy this one over the Halloween season.

The Devil of Kreuzberg (2015)

Ah, Linda! Sweet. Devoted. Loyal. But wait! Her last name is Karnstein! Admirers of Hammer horror films know what that means. Linda is exotic, beautiful, and of course... cursed. Today we look at 2015's "The Devil of Kreuzberg," a film from Germany and directed by Alexander Bakshaev. Atmospheric with a soundtrack from a Lucio Fulci horror film, after watching this film you will feel compelled to smear blood somewhere.

Absolutely devoted to Jakob (Ludwig Reuter), Linda (Sandra Bourdonnec) is 100 % in love. An author mired in a prolonged slump, Jakob appears to lead an imprisoned existence. He isn't as into Linda as Linda is into him. In Jakob, Linda has, what she believes, a key into the world of light. In Linda, Jakob believes death awaits. Enter Kurt (Suleyman Yuceer). Kurt and Jakob are best friends. These two perhaps should be more than friends, but the conventions of western civilization dictate that they should just be good friends. Just as well. Kurt is problematic. He pays off his debts to gangsters by performing hits on those who don't pay debts.

Now fate knocks on the door. Linda fights her destiny (...remember, she is a Karnstein). Jakob, sensing Linda is not quite mortal (...how many of us are?) turns to his assassin friend. Kurt, a very sensitive assassin, fights the path he is going down...but his best friend has asked a favor. This will all play out in spooky cemetery scenes, a pursuit through a subway station with pseudo pagan designs, and dark and damp streets of Berlin. No spoilers here.

Fans of horror know not to date someone named Karnstein. No doubt Jakob wasn't a horror writer. No matter...these three were brought together, we sense, by much more than free will. This relatively short film (49 minutes) goes at a brisk pace and is always on edge. Very well acted and masterfully directed, "The Devil of Kreuzberg" shouldn't be missed. The ending will chill you, and perhaps keep you up at night fighting those same nightmares Jakob battled.

Afterward

Of all the horror sub-genres, vampire films are the most popular on *Zisi Emporium for B Movies*. The 38 films filling this book are some of my favorite vampire movies. In a traditional sense, there is usually a defined good and a defined evil. In more recent years, the vampire, on occasion, has taken the role of the protagonist. Either way, vampires do make terrific fiction. Perhaps one day I will do a book on major release vampire films such as Tod Browning's "Dracula," and the five "Underworld" films. For now, B films, straight-to-DVD, obscure foreign treasures, and pseudo exploitation drive-in classics will have to do.

By all means, if there is a vampire film not included in these pages, which you wish was, send me a Twitter message at @cjzisi. I will do all I can to find the film and review it on my blog.

19672015R00056

Printed in Great Britain
by Amazon